TALES OF
Sherlock Holmes
Retold Timeless Classics

Perfection Learning®

Retold by L. L. Owens

Editor: Susan Sexton
Illustrator: Greg Nemec

For information, contact
Perfection Learning® Corporation,
1000 North Second Avenue, P.O. Box 500
Logan, Iowa 51546-1099.
Phone: 1-800-831-4190 • Fax: 1-712-644-2392

Paperback ISBN 0-7891-2863-2
Cover Craft® ISBN 0-7807-7857-x
Printed in the U.S.A.

Sir Arthur Conan Doyle
(1859–1930)

Arthur Conan Doyle was born on May 22, 1859, in Edinburgh, Scotland. He began his career as a medical doctor. But writing had always been his secret passion.

Doyle's medical practice eventually fell on hard times. So he began writing stories to earn extra money. Before long, he was the highest-paid writer of his time. And he left the medical profession behind.

Doyle's most famous character was Sherlock Holmes. The brilliant London detective first appeared in *A Study in Scarlet* in 1887.

Stories from *The Adventures of Sherlock Holmes* appeared in *Strand Magazine* in 1891 and 1892. "The Speckled Band" and "The Redheaded League" are part of this collection. "The Priory School" and "The Three Students" are from *The Return of Sherlock Holmes*.

The public adored the sly, gifted Holmes. The great sleuth was also a boxer, chemist, composer, swordsman, and violinist.

Holmes and his friend Dr. John H. Watson spent many years at 221B Baker Street. And an endless stream of fascinating people visited their apartment. Each character was involved in a mystery of some sort. And each one desperately needed—and received—Holmes' help.

Watson was always on hand to assist with the adventures. He also kept detailed records on each case. In later stories, Watson no longer lived with Holmes. But he always served as the stories' narrator.

Surprisingly, Doyle himself was not very fond of Holmes. He felt that writing about the detective kept him from doing more serious writing. So he once wrote a story in which Holmes died. But the public protested. And Doyle brought Holmes back to life in his next tale!

Other works by Sir Arthur Conan Doyle include *The Hound of the Baskervilles* and *The Lost World*. He died of a heart attack on July 7, 1930.

Table of Contents

The Speckled Band

I WOKE UP early. Sherlock Holmes was standing by the side of my bed. I blinked up at him in surprise.

"Very sorry to wake you, Watson," Holmes said. "But we have a client. A young lady is waiting in the parlor. I thought you would like to follow the case."

"Yes, thank you. I would," I replied.

The Lady States Her Case

Moments later, Holmes and I were in the parlor.

"Good morning, madam," said Holmes cheerily. "My name is Sherlock Holmes. This is Dr. Watson."

The young lady looked frightened. "I have no one to turn to," she said. "I hope you can help me."

"Please go on," said Holmes.

"My name is Helen Stoner," the young lady began. "I live with my stepfather. He is the last of the Roylotts of Stoke Moran."

Holmes nodded. "I know the name."

"The family was once very rich," Helen said. "Now the only thing left is the 200-year-old house. My stepfather became a doctor to earn a living. He even had a large practice in Calcutta.

"But he killed a man there in a fit of rage," she revealed. "And he served time in prison. Afterward, he returned to England. And to the family home."

Helen twisted a handkerchief in her hands as she continued. "Dr. Roylott married my mother. She was the former Mrs. Stoner. My father had died the year before. My twin sister, Julia, and I were only two years old.

"Eight years ago, our mother died. She left behind enough money to provide for all three of us. At least until Julia and I got married," she added. "Then the rest of the money would be divided between Julia and me. Dr. Roylott has always managed the money for us."

Helen took a deep breath.

"After Mother's passing," she continued, "a terrible change came over Dr. Roylott. He rarely left the house. And when he did, he often started fights with people for no reason. Also, he began collecting wild animals. He has a cheetah and a baboon.

"Julia died just two years ago," Helen said sadly. "She was 30. It is her death that I wish to speak to you about."

"Details, please," pressed Holmes.

"I'll do my best," replied Helen. "The house is very old and very large. Most of it is shut off.

"The bedrooms and the parlor are on the first floor," she explained. "The first bedroom is Dr. Roylott's. The second was my sister's. And the third is my own. All the windows face the lawn. The rooms are not connected. But they all open into the same hall. Is that clear?"

"Perfectly so," said Holmes.

"That night, Dr. Roylott went to his room early," Helen continued. "But he did not go right to sleep. Julia could tell. She smelled his cigar smoke.

"Anyway, Julia and I sat in my room. And we chatted about her upcoming wedding. It was just two weeks away."

"Later, Julia rose to leave," Helen said as she dropped her eyes. She looked at the twisted handkerchief in her hands.

"Julia asked whether I had ever heard a whistle in the dead of night," Helen continued. "I said that I had not. Then she revealed that she had. Each night for the past week. And always at about three o'clock in the morning."

Helen looked up. "Soon, she was back in her bedroom. And I heard her key turn in the lock."

"Indeed," said Holmes. "Did you always lock yourselves in at night?"

"Always," replied Helen.

"Why?" asked Holmes.

"We were afraid of the animals," Helen said. "They roamed the grounds at night. So we didn't feel safe unless our doors were locked."

"I see," nodded Holmes. "Please finish your tale."

"Well, I couldn't sleep," Helen continued. "The wind was howling. And the rain was beating against the windows. Suddenly, I heard Julia scream. I rushed into the hallway. That's when I heard a low whistle, then a clanging sound. It was as if a piece of metal had fallen.

"Julia opened her door. She was groping for help. And I ran to her side. But she fell to the ground. She was in dreadful pain.

"Julia shrieked, 'The band! The speckled band!' And she pointed toward the doctor's room.

"I then cried out for my stepfather. But when he reached Julia's side, she was dead."

"One moment," interrupted Holmes. "Are you sure about this whistle? And the clanging sound? Could you swear to it?"

"Yes," Helen assured.

"Was your sister dressed?" Holmes asked.

"No," Helen replied. "She was in her nightgown. And she was holding a used match."

"That is important, Watson," said Holmes. "Remember that. For it shows that Julia had struck a light and looked about. Probably after hearing the whistle."

Holmes turned back to Helen. "Tell me, my dear," he said. "Did another doctor examine Julia's body?"

"Yes," Helen replied. "But he couldn't find the cause of death. It is certain that Julia had been quite alone in her room. And she had suffered no injuries."

"What about poison?" I asked.

"No traces of it were found," Helen said.

"Did you understand Julia's last words?" asked Holmes. "About a speckled band?"

"I'm not sure. Sometimes I think that it meant nothing," Helen said slowly. "That perhaps Julia had gone mad. But other times, well . . . I don't know."

"Please do share your thoughts," said Holmes. "Every small fact helps solve the puzzle."

"Very well," Helen agreed. "My stepfather allowed a friendly band of gypsies to camp on the estate. Many of them wore spotted handkerchiefs on their heads. So sometimes I think Julia's words—'the speckled band'—might have meant the gypsies."

Holmes nodded his head.

"Fascinating," he said. "Is there more?"

"Well, as I said, two years have passed," Helen continued. "A month ago, a dear man asked for my hand in marriage. We are to wed in the spring.

"A few days ago, my stepfather ordered some repairs in my bedroom. So I had to move into Julia's old room.

"Last night, I heard a low whistle," she said fearfully. "The same one I heard the night of

Julia's death. Imagine my fright! I sprang up and lit the lamp. But I could see nothing out of the ordinary.

"I was too shaken to go back to bed. So I dressed. As soon as it was daylight, I slipped out of the house. And I made my way to you."

"A wise move," noted Holmes. "But have you told me everything?"

"Yes," Helen answered cautiously.

"Are you sure?" Holmes pressed. "I feel that you are protecting your stepfather."

"What do you mean?" asked Helen.

Holmes pushed back Helen's black lace sleeve. On her wrist were the purple marks of four large fingers and a thumb.

"He has hurt you," said Holmes.

Helen blushed and lowered her eyes. "He is a hard man," she said. "He doesn't know his own strength."

There was a long silence.

Finally, Holmes said, "All right, then. We have not a moment to lose. May Watson and I see the rooms in your home today? Without your stepfather's knowledge?"

"Yes—he will be away all day," Helen said.

"Excellent!" exclaimed Holmes. "When shall we arrive?"

"I shall return on the 12 o'clock train," Helen answered. "I'll look forward to seeing you in the early afternoon."

With that, Helen glided from the room.

Holmes leaned far back in his chair. "What do you think of it all, Watson?" he asked.

I thought for a moment. Then I replied. "It seems to be a rather dark business."

"Indeed, Watson," Holmes agreed. "Let us review the facts as we know them—"

Just then, a huge man appeared in the doorway.

"Which of you is Holmes?" he asked.

"I am, sir," replied Holmes.

"I am Dr. Grimesby Roylott," the large man announced. "Of Stoke Moran."

"Dr. Roylott," said Holmes calmly. "Please sit down."

"I will do nothing of the kind!" boomed Roylott. "My stepdaughter has been here. I followed her. I demand that you stay out of my affairs!"

Roylott walked to the fireplace. He seized the poker. And easily he bent it into a curve.

"I could do this to you!" he snarled. He hurled the poker into the fireplace. Then he stormed out of the room.

"What a pleasant fellow," said Holmes, laughing. Then he grew serious. "I hope Helen will not suffer for this. And now, Watson, we shall order breakfast. Afterward, I shall do a bit of research."

A Clear Motive

Holmes returned at one o'clock. He was dressed in his best tweeds.

"My morning's work was fruitful," he declared.

He showed me a copy of Mrs. Roylott's will. It showed why Dr. Roylott might wish to prevent his stepdaughters from marrying. If they remained single, he would continue receiving a nice monthly sum. With which he was supposed to provide for the young ladies.

And if the sisters died? Then Dr. Roylott would inherit all his late wife's money!

Holmes gathered up the papers. And he put on his traveling hat and cape. "I'll call a driver," he said. "Time is running out. Especially since the doctor knows we are involved."

"I'm ready," I said. Though I wasn't quite sure what we were getting into.

"Watson?" asked Holmes.

"Yes?" I replied.

"Why don't you slip your revolver into your pocket," Holmes suggested. "Besides your toothbrush, that should be all you need."

Inspecting Stoke Moran

Before I knew it, we were approaching the Roylott estate.

"Look there!" said Holmes.

"That is Stoke Moran," stated the driver. "Dr. Grimesby Roylott lives there."

"Indeed. We need to get to the house," explained Holmes.

The driver replied, "Then I'd best let you off here. You'll find it shorter to get there by the path over the fields. It's right over there. Where the lady is walking."

"Yes," agreed Holmes. "I think we shall do as you suggest."

We got off and paid our fare.

"Good afternoon, Helen!" Holmes called out.

"I am so glad to see you!" she cried. "All has turned out well. Dr. Roylott has gone to town. He will not be back until this evening."

"We have had the pleasure of meeting the doctor," said Holmes.

"He followed me?" Helen asked.

"So it appears," said Holmes. "Now kindly take us to the rooms we need to examine."

Holmes briefly walked up and down the lawn. He studied the windows. Then he pointed to one. "This," he observed, "belongs to your old room. The center one belonged to your sister. And the next one is Dr. Roylott's room. Correct?"

"Correct," Helen replied. "But I am now sleeping in the middle one. There is work being done to my room."

"But I don't see any great need for repairs," I noted.

"There is none," said Helen coldly. "I think it was just an excuse to move me from my room."

"Now, Helen," instructed Holmes. "Please go into your room and close your shutters. Use the iron bar too—just as you do at night."

Helen did so. Holmes tried to force the shutter open. But he couldn't.

"Hmm!" said he, scratching his chin. "No one could pass these bolted shutters. There isn't even a slit. If there were, perhaps a knife could pass through and raise the iron bar. But it's not possible."

With that, Holmes led the way inside. He refused to examine the third bedroom. So we went to the second. That's the one that Helen now occupied. And the one in which Julia had died.

Holmes sat silently in a corner. He took in every detail of the room.

"That bell?" he asked at last. He pointed to a thick rope that hung beside the bed. "Where does the sound go?"

"It goes to the housekeeper's room," said Helen.

"It looks newer than the other things," Holmes observed.

"It is," explained Helen. "It was only put there a couple of years ago."

"Your sister asked for it, I suppose?" Homes inquired.

"No. She had no use for it," Helen stated. "We always did things for ourselves."

Holmes took the rope in his hand. He gave it a sharp tug.

"It's a fake," he said. "It's not even attached to a wire."

"I never noticed that before," said Helen, amazed.

"Very strange!" muttered Holmes. "And look at that vent over there. It must open into your stepfather's room."

"The vent is also new," said Helèn. "It was added about the same time as the bell rope."

We moved on to Dr. Roylott's room. It was plainly furnished. And it had a large safe in it.

Holmes tapped the safe. "What's in here?" he asked.

"Papers," answered Helen.

"Oh! You have seen inside?" Homes asked.

"Only once, years ago," Helen replied. "I just remember that it was full of papers."

"There isn't a cat in it, for example?" asked Holmes.

"No!" she exclaimed. "What a strange idea!"

"Well, look at this!" Holmes pointed to a saucer of milk. It rested on top of the safe.

Next he examined the seat of a wooden chair. "Clearly someone stands on this," he declared. Indeed, the seat dipped in the middle.

"Ah!" Holmes said. "What do you make of that, Watson?"

Holmes was looking at a small whip. It hung on one corner of the bed. The lash was tied into a loop.

"It's a common enough whip," I offered. "I wonder why it's tied."

"I cannot imagine," Holmes said. "I have seen enough now, Helen. With your permission, we shall walk upon the lawn."

We three walked up and down the lawn. Holmes was silent. He was deep in thought.

At last, he spoke to Helen. "You must do exactly as I say. This is essential to your very life."

"I'll do as you say," she vowed.

"In the first place, Watson and I must spend the night," said Holmes. "In your room."

Helen and I both gasped in surprise.

"Yes, it must be so," Holmes said evenly. "Let me explain." Then he pointed to a building. It was on the other side of the path we'd taken. "Is that an inn over there?"

"Yes. That is the Crown Inn," Helen said.

"Very good. Would your windows be visible from there?" Holmes asked.

"Certainly," Helen replied.

"All right, then. The minute your stepfather returns, say you feel ill," instructed Holmes. "Then go straight to your room."

Helen nodded. And Holmes continued.

"Wait until you hear him retire for the night. Open your shutters. Undo the latch. And put your lamp there as a signal.

"Then leave the room quietly. And go to your old room for the night. Can you do that?"

"Oh, yes," Helen answered excitedly. "Easily. But what will you do?"

"We shall spend the night in your room," replied Holmes. "And we shall find the source of this whistle."

"Tell me something, Mr. Holmes," said Helen.

"What is it?" Holmes asked.

"I sense that you have already decided what is going on," she said. "Is that true?"

"Perhaps," Holmes replied mysteriously.

"Then—please!" cried Helen. "Tell me what caused my sister's death."

"I'm afraid I cannot say," said Holmes. "Not until I have proof. And now we must leave you. But you shall soon be safe. And you shall have your answers."

Sherlock Holmes and I got rooms at the Crown Inn. From our window we could see Stoke Moran. At dusk, we saw Dr. Roylott arrive home.

"You know," said Holmes. "I knew that we

would find a vent between the rooms. Even before we came to Stoke Moran."

"My dear Holmes!" I cried. "How?"

"Helen said that Julia could smell Dr. Roylott's cigar smoke," Holmes explained. "So there had to be at least a small connection between the rooms. And I thought of a vent."

"But what harm can there be in a vent?" I asked.

"A good question," Holmes admitted. "But think of the order of events. First, a vent is made. Then a cord is hung. And finally, a lady who sleeps in the bed dies."

"I do not see the connection," I shrugged. But I knew that Holmes would explain it to me.

"Did you notice anything odd about that bed?" he asked.

"No," I confessed.

"It was clamped to the floor," Holmes revealed. "The lady could not move her bed. It must always be near the vent and the rope."

"Holmes!" I cried. "I see what you are hinting at. We are only just in time! We must prevent another horrible crime."

The Suspense Builds

At about 11 o'clock, a light shone through Helen's window.

"That is our signal," said Holmes.

A moment later, Holmes and I were out on the dark road. We soon reached the lawn. We were about to enter through the window. But an ugly creature ran from behind a bush. Then it disappeared again into the darkness.

"Did you see it?" I whispered. My heart beat wildly in my chest.

Holmes was startled too. Then he chuckled quietly and put his lips to my ear.

"That was the baboon," he whispered.

Next, we slipped into the bedroom. We both took off our shoes. Holmes carefully closed the shutters. He moved the lamp to the table. And he looked around the room. Nothing had changed since the daytime.

Holmes whispered into my ear, "The least sound would ruin our plans."

I nodded.

"We must sit without light," he said. "Roylott might see it through the vent."

I nodded again.

"Have your pistol ready," Holmes

whispered. "I will sit on the side of the bed. You sit in that chair."

Holmes had brought with him a long, thin cane. He placed it on the bed beside him. He laid a box of matches and a candle next to it. Then he turned down the lamp.

We waited in absolute silence. And total darkness. From outside came the occasional cry of a night bird.

Suddenly, a gleam of light showed through the vent. It disappeared immediately.

Then came a strong smell. It was of burning oil. And heated metal. Someone in the next room had lit a lantern. The smell grew stronger.

Then we heard a very soft sound. It sounded like steam escaping from a kettle.

Holmes sprang from the bed. He struck a match. And he lashed at the bell rope with his cane.

"Watson!" Holmes yelled. "Do you see it?"

But I saw nothing. I'd heard a low, clear whistle. But I could not tell what Holmes was trying to hit.

Holmes stopped lashing. And he gazed up at the vent. We heard a horrible cry.

"What has happened?" I gasped.

"It is all over," Holmes answered. "Grab your pistol."

With a grave face, he lit the lamp. And then we walked to Roylott's room.

Holmes knocked twice. There was no reply, so we entered.

On the table stood a lantern. The shutter was half open. And a beam of light shone upon the safe. The door to the safe was open.

Dr. Roylott sat on the wooden chair beside the table. Across his lap lay the whip. He was perfectly still.

"The band! The speckled band!" cried Holmes.

A strange yellow band—with brownish speckles—was wound around Roylott's head.

The speckled band began to move! It showed us its diamond-shaped head! And its puffed neck!

"A swamp adder!" cried Holmes. "The deadliest snake in India. Its bite causes instant death. Roylott didn't feel a thing."

As Holmes spoke, he picked up the whip. He threw the noose round the snake's neck. And he threw it into the safe. Then he locked it up.

And such are the true facts of the death of Dr. Grimesby Roylott.

The Pieces Fit

We broke the sad news to Helen. And we put her on the morning train to her aunt's house.

The police concluded that the doctor had died while playing with a dangerous pet.

Holmes explained everything as we traveled home.

To him, it was clear that nothing could have entered her room. Not from the window. Not from the door.

So Holmes had turned his attention to the vent. And to the bell rope, which hung down to the bed.

Of course, he'd discovered that the bell rope was a fake. And that the bed was clamped to the floor.

Holmes then suspected that the rope was there as a bridge. So that something could pass through the vent. And drop down to the bed.

"The idea of a snake instantly occurred to me," Holmes stated. "Especially since the doctor already had other creatures from India. The doctor knew that the snake's poison could not be detected. And he knew how fast it would kill his victims."

"But weren't there bite marks?" I asked.

"Certainly. But Roylott took that chance. And he won. The other doctor didn't notice them."

"What do you make of the whistle?" I asked.

"Ah," said Holmes. "Roylott used that cleverly. You see, he had to recall the snake. Before Julia or Helen could see it in the morning light. So he trained it.

"He probably used the milk we saw. The snake would hear the whistle. And it would slither up the rope. Crawl through the vent. And make its way to the milk," Holmes explained. "That was its reward!"

"That all makes sense," I said. "But why did Julia hear the whistle on several nights?"

"It's quite simple, really," replied Holmes. "Roylott knew he could make the snake crawl down the rope. And even land on the bed. But the snake wouldn't necessarily bite the person sleeping there. Obviously, Julia escaped the poisonous fangs several times. By sheer chance! But finally, the snake bit her."

He continued. "In any event, I felt sure about what had happened. So once I heard the snake hiss, I lit the light. And I attacked it."

"And that drove it back through the vent!" I cried. "I've said it before, Holmes. And I'll say it again. You're brilliant! Yet I have one more small question."

"Yes?" Holmes asked.

"You studied the wooden chair in Roylott's room. The seat was bowed. Was that a clue?" I asked.

"Most definitely!" exclaimed Holmes. "I reached an easy conclusion there. And that was that Roylott often stood on that chair. It's the only explanation of the seat's condition."

This puzzled me. "Why on earth would he stand on the chair?"

"How else could he reach the vent, old boy?" Holmes explained.

We rode on in silence for a while. And I realized that all the pieces fit.

The metallic clanging heard by Helen made sense. It was no doubt caused when Roylott slammed shut the safe's door. This, of course, locked in the deadly snake.

At length, Holmes laughed.

"What is it?" I asked.

"I was thinking," Holmes replied. "My attack on the adder no doubt made it angry. So it sank its fangs into the first person it saw."

"Roylott," I said.

"One might say that I am indirectly to blame for Dr. Roylott's death," Holmes said.

"And I cannot say that I am sorry for it."

"The man was a fiend," I said. "Roylott was quite ready to use the snake on a second victim. You saved Helen's life."

"Indeed, Watson," said Holmes. "Indeed."

And with that, our carriage pulled to a stop. We were back at 221B Baker Street. Where new adventures would surely find us.

THE
REDHEADED
LEAGUE

I CALLED UPON Sherlock Holmes. He was talking with a gentleman. The man had fiery red hair.

"Welcome, my dear Dr. Watson," Holmes said.

"This gentleman," Holmes explained to his guest, "has helped me with many cases."

Holmes' guest, Mr. Wilson, greeted me politely.

"Show Watson the newspaper ad," Holmes said to Wilson. "That will bring him up to speed."

I took the paper from Wilson.

It was from the *Morning Chronicle.*

> **TO ALL REDHEADED MEN:**
>
> THERE IS AN OPEN SPOT IN THE **REDHEADED LEAGUE.** PAY IS 4 POUNDS A WEEK. ALL **REDHEADED** MEN OVER 21 MAY APPLY. COME TO THE OFFICES ON FLEET STREET. MONDAY—11:00 A.M.

"What on earth?" I asked.

"It is curious, isn't it?" Holmes chuckled. "Now, Mr. Wilson. Please tell your story. From the beginning."

"I have a small business in the city," Wilson began. "I used to have two assistants. But now I can only keep one."

"What is his name?" asked Holmes.

"Vincent Spaulding," said Wilson. "He works hard. I am very lucky to have him. For he willingly works for half the regular pay. He has some odd habits though. He snaps pictures constantly. Then he dives into the cellar to develop them. He spends hours down there every day. Other than that, he's a good worker."

"Go on," prompted Holmes.

"Spaulding showed me this ad two months ago," Wilson continued. "That's when it ran. I thought it might be a joke. But he claimed he'd heard of the Redheaded League."

"What did he know about it?" I asked.

"He said it had been started by an American millionaire," Wilson explained. "The man had left money in his will. The money's purpose was to provide easy jobs for other redheads.

"The pay wasn't great. But it would be extra since Spaulding could watch the store for me."

"So you decided to check it out," prompted Holmes.

"Yes," said Wilson. Then he described what he'd found.

Apparently, swarms of redheaded men had flooded Fleet Street. They lined up around the block. But somehow, Spaulding pushed Wilson to the front. And they went into the office.

A man with blazing red hair greeted them. He took one look at Wilson and shook his hand.

"My name is Duncan Ross. And you meet every requirement," he said.

Then, just to be sure, he tugged at Wilson's hair. "We have to be careful," he asserted. "We have twice been fooled by wigs. And once by paint! That settles it. You have won the position! When can you start?"

"What are the hours? And what exactly is the job?" asked Wilson.

"The hours are 10:00 a.m. to 2:00 p.m. The pay is four pounds per week. And the job is copying the *Encyclopedia Britannica,*" said Ross.

He went on. "You must stay in the office the whole time. If you leave, you lose your position."

Wilson thought it sounded so easy! He said he could be ready the next morning.

When Wilson arrived, everything was ready for him. Duncan Ross was there to start him off. He sat him at a table with pen and paper. And he gave him the first volume of the encyclopedia. Then he left.

At the end of the day, he came back and checked on Wilson's progress. And he seemed quite pleased with his work.

Wilson concluded his tale. "This went on day after day, Mr. Holmes. For eight weeks. Until this morning. That's when it ended. When I arrived, there was a note tacked to the door. I looked for Duncan Ross. But the landlord told me there was no such person. When I described Mr. Ross, the landlord knew him. But under a different name. He said that he'd paid his rent on the office and left this morning. With no forwarding address, of course."

He showed us the note.

> To Mr. Jabez Wilson:
> The Redheaded League has
> dissolved. Please go home
> and don't come back!
> —October 9, 1890

Sherlock Holmes and I studied this blunt announcement. And then we looked at Mr. Wilson's sad face. I regret to say that the two of us burst out laughing.

"I see nothing funny about this!" cried our client.

"No, no!" exclaimed Holmes. "I'm dreadfully sorry. We would love to take your case. It's just so unusual. But I assure you that we shall take the matter seriously. This is a seemingly harmless—and highly unusual—injustice. But that probably points to a larger misdeed. No doubt something criminal."

"I thank you," said Wilson. "I do wish to get to the bottom of this awful prank."

"I have one or two questions for you," said Holmes. "How long has your assistant been with you?"

"About three months," replied Wilson.

"Was he the only applicant?" Holmes asked.

"No," Wilson said. "I had a dozen."

"Why did you pick him?" I asked.

"Because he was handy and would work cheaply," Wilson said.

"Describe this Vincent Spaulding," directed Holmes. He was clearly intrigued.

"He's a small man," Wilson replied. "Very quick in his ways. He is over 30. But he looks quite boyish. And he has a large white scar on his forehead."

Holmes sat up in his chair. "I thought as much!" he cried. "That will do for now, Mr. Wilson. Today is Saturday. I hope that by Monday the case will be solved."

Mr. Wilson showed himself out.

"There's a concert at the St. James this afternoon," Holmes remarked. "Shall we go?"

"Certainly," I said.

"Excellent," he replied. "We'll walk through the city first. I'd like to gather some clues on this case."

THE SCENE OF THE CRIME?

Soon, we were in front of Mr. Wilson's shop. It was on the ground floor of his home. And it was closed for the weekend.

Sherlock Holmes looked it over. Then he walked slowly up the street and back. He took note of the other houses.

In front of Wilson's house, Holmes thumped the pavement with his walking stick. Then he knocked on the door. A bright-looking young fellow opened it. I knew he must be Wilson's assistant—Spaulding.

Holmes said hello, then asked a question. "Could you tell me how to get to the St. James from here?"

"Third right, fourth left," answered the assistant. And he promptly closed the door.

"Smart fellow," observed Holmes as we walked away.

"Evidently," I said, "you suspect him. Do you think he is behind the Redheaded League scam?"

"I am quite sure of it," answered Holmes. "Did you notice the knees of his trousers?"

"No," I said. "Are they important?"

"Very," said Holmes. "They were ragged.

As I suspected they would be. Now I'd like to explore the area."

Behind Wilson's house was a row of businesses. Holmes took note of them all. There was Mortimer's and the newspaper shop. The City Bank and the Vegetarian Restaurant. And the depot.

"And now, Watson, we've done our work," said Holmes merrily. "It's time we had some play. Let's have a sandwich and a cup of coffee. Then it's off to the concert."

Later, we emerged from the St. James onto the busy street. We'd heard a lovely violin concert.

"Meet me back at Baker Street. Tonight at ten," Holmes remarked.

"Baker Street at ten," I promised.

"There may be some danger," cautioned Holmes. "So bring your revolver."

Holmes waved his hand and turned on his heel. Then he disappeared into the crowd.

A HUNTING PARTY

I arrived at my friend's rooms promptly at ten. Holmes was meeting with two men.

"Watson!" he announced. "I think you know Mr. Jones—of Scotland Yard? Let me introduce you to Mr. Merryweather. He is the director of the City Bank."

"How do you do," I nodded.

"We're after John Clay," said Jones.

"John Clay?" I asked. "The name rings a bell. But I cannot place it."

"He's a murderer, a thief, a smasher, and a forger," said Jones. "I've been on his track for years."

Holmes' eyes flashed. "We shall catch him tonight. It is past ten, gentlemen—quite time that we started."

Holmes grabbed his coat and hat. Then he snatched his hunting crop from the corner. "One never knows," he remarked.

We all took a carriage to Wilson's neighborhood. We were let out near the bank.

Mr. Merryweather swiftly and quietly led us to the bank's cellar.

Holmes fell to the floor at once. With a lantern and a magnifying lens, he examined the cracks between the stones.

"We have at least an hour before us," Holmes deduced. "For they won't take any steps until Wilson is safely in bed. Then they will not lose a minute."

"What are they after?" I asked.

"Our French gold," whispered Merryweather. "We have been storing a good deal of it these past three months. And we have received warnings that Clay might come after it."

"Merryweather," whispered Holmes, "please put the screen over that lantern."

"And sit in the dark?" asked Merryweather.

"I am afraid so," said Holmes. "These are daring men. They may harm us unless we are careful. I shall stand behind this crate. And you conceal yourselves behind those. When I flash a light upon them, grab them. And Watson—if they fire, shoot them down."

Holmes placed a screen over his lantern. This left us in pitch darkness. The smell of hot metal assured us that the light was still there. That it was ready to flash on at a moment's notice.

"They have but one way out," whispered Holmes. "That is back through Wilson's house into the street. Did you do as I asked, Jones?"

"Yes," Jones replied. "I have an inspector and two officers waiting at the front door."

"Good," said Holmes. "Then we must be silent and wait."

We waited for an hour and a quarter. But it seemed much longer. I was very tense. And all I could hear were the sounds of others breathing in the darkness.

HOLMES NABS THE CROOKS

Suddenly, I saw a glimmer of light.

At first, it was only a spark on the stone pavement. Then one of the broad, white stones turned over. It left a gaping hole through which streamed more light.

A clean-cut, boyish face popped through the hole. He climbed through. Then he helped a companion do the same. His companion had a pale face and a shock of very red hair.

"It's all clear," he whispered. "Have you the chisel? And the bags?"

Sherlock Holmes seized the first intruder by the collar. The other dived back through the hole.

The thief reached for a revolver. But Holmes slapped the man's wrist with his hunting crop. And the pistol clinked upon the stone floor.

"It's no use, John Clay," said Holmes. "You have no chance at all."

"So I see," Clay answered coolly. "I fancy that my pal is all right, though."

"Wrong again!" Holmes exclaimed. "Three men are waiting for him at the door."

"Then I must compliment you," said Clay.

"And I you," Holmes allowed. "Your redheaded idea was very fresh. Very effective. But now you're off to the police station. Take him, Jones."

"Thank you, Mr. Holmes!" cried Mr. Merryweather.

"Not at all," replied the great detective.

THE MYSTERY UNRAVELS

As usual, Holmes filled in the blanks over a late-night snack at Baker Street.

"You see, Watson," he began, "it was obvious from the beginning."

"Really!" I laughed.

"Oh, quite," he said. "The Redheaded League was merely a cover. Someone wanted Mr. Wilson out of the way for several hours each day.

"Clay no doubt thought of the scheme by chance. Probably when he noticed that Wilson's red hair matched his friend's," Holmes explained. "This happened after he had already been hired at Wilson's shop."

"But how could you guess what the league was meant to cover?" I asked.

"Wilson's business was small. So they didn't want to rob him," Holmes said. "It had to be, then, something out of the house. What could it be? Then I thought of the time the assistant spent in the cellar. And there was the end of this tangled clue."

Holmes paced the floor as he told the rest of the story.

"From Wilson's description, I knew his assistant wasn't really Vincent Spaulding. I knew he was the scoundrel John Clay. He is one of the smartest and most daring criminals in London. Think about it, Watson."

"I am," I assured him. "But please do explain."

"He was disappearing into the cellar for hours each day. For months on end. What was he doing?" Holmes wondered. "I could think of nothing. Except that he was digging a tunnel to some other building.

"When we visited the scene, I beat upon the pavement. I was seeing whether Wilson's cellar stretched out in front or behind. This told me it was not in front."

"And what about the young man's pants?" I asked. "Why were they important?"

"I all but told you, old boy!" Holmes exclaimed. "The knees were worn and stained. Clearly, he spent hours working on his knees. The explanation, of course, is that he was digging. But for what?

"So I walked around the corner. I saw that the City Bank building rested against our friend's shop. And I felt that I had solved the case.

"When you left me, I called upon Jones at Scotland Yard. Then I called upon Mr. Merryweather."

I was awed by his powers of deduction.

"How did you know they would make their attempt tonight?" I asked.

"Well, they had closed their Redheaded League offices. They no longer needed Wilson to stay away while they dug. That was a sign that they had finished their tunnel. But they had to use it soon. Robbing the bank on Saturday would give them the weekend to escape. It was a gamble. But I felt sure that they would strike tonight."

"You reasoned it out beautifully," I exclaimed. "As always."

"It saves me from boredom," he answered, yawning. "I struggle to escape from boredom every day. These little mysteries help me do so."

"Then it is a good arrangement," I said. "Your mysteries help you. And you help others."

Holmes shrugged. "Well, perhaps it is of some little use. As someone once said—

" 'A man's work is more important than the man himself!' "

THE PRIORY SCHOOL

SHERLOCK HOLMES AND I took an early train to Mackleton. Thorneycroft Huxtable, Ph.D., had sent for Holmes.

Dr. Huxtable worked at the Priory School for Boys. One of the students had been kidnapped!

When we arrived at the school, Holmes introduced us.

"May I present Dr. Watson," Holmes said. "He often helps with my cases."

"Pleased to make your acquaintance," said Dr. Huxtable. Then he filled us in.

"You know of the Duke of Holdernesse," he began.

"Of course," said Holmes.

"The duke's son is missing," said Huxtable. "He's ten years old. Arthur's his name. He's been gone for three days."

"Three days?" bellowed Holmes. "What have the police found? And why was this not reported in the *Globe?*"

"The duke wishes to keep it quiet. The police have not been told. But I could keep still no longer. So I sent for you. I'm worried about the boy!"

"Dear me," I said.

" 'Dear me' is right, Watson," sighed Holmes. He shook his head. "Who knows what might have happened in three days. We'll be lucky to find any clues to follow! But please, Huxtable. Do continue."

Huxtable explained everything. Arthur's mother and father were not getting along. So the duchess was living in the south of France.

Arthur missed his mother. The duke thought a term at the Priory School would cheer him up.

So Arthur was enrolled for the summer term. He quickly made friends. In fact, he had been quite happy.

He was last seen on the evening of May 13. He had gone to bed. But the next morning, he was gone. He had dressed in his school uniform.

"We soon found that someone else was missing," said Huxtable. "Heidegger—the German teacher. But he had apparently left only partly dressed."

"Why do you say so?" Holmes asked.

"Simple," replied Huxtable. "His shirt and socks were lying on the floor. And his bed had been slept in. He must have left in a hurry. His bicycle is also gone. There are no traces of him. Or the boy."

Sherlock Holmes had listened carefully. He again expressed his complaint. "So three days have been wasted. There is no excuse for that. The boy may be in grave danger. Has anyone requested ransom from the duke?"

"No," replied Huxtable.

"What do you say, Watson?" said Holmes. "Shall we take the case?"

"I see no choice in the matter," I replied.

"Nor do I," he said. "Huxtable, did Arthur have a bicycle? Or was another bicycle missing?"

"No," said Huxtable.

"One more question," added Holmes. "Did anyone visit the boy the day before he disappeared?"

"No," said Huxtable again.

"Did he get any letters?" inquired Holmes.

"Yes," Huxtable said. "One from his father."

"When had he received a letter before that?" asked Holmes.

"He hadn't. He's only been here two weeks," explained Huxtable.

"You see the point of my questions," explained Holmes. "The boy may have been carried off by force. But I think that he left on his own. He has had no visitors. So perhaps someone wrote to him and told him to leave."

"I see," said Huxtable.

"Let us visit the duke," said Holmes.

■ Holmes Questions the Duke

It was already dark when Holmes, Dr. Huxtable, and I reached Holdernesse Hall.

"The duke and Mr. Wilder are in the study," said the butler.

Mr. Wilder, a young man, was the duke's private secretary. The butler introduced us all.

The duke was surprised to see the famous Sherlock Holmes.

"Huxtable! I thought we were keeping this quiet," said the duke. "Yet here stands a famous detective."

"Yes, sir," explained Huxtable. "But we are getting nowhere without help. Holmes and Watson won't speak to the papers."

"Certainly not," promised Holmes. "We are merely interested in the safe return of the boy."

"As you like, Mr. Holmes," the duke explained gruffly. "Mr. Wilder and I will help in any way we can."

"Splendid," explained Holmes. "Have you come to any conclusions about your son's mysterious disappearance?"

"No, sir, I have not," said the duke.

"Do you suspect the duchess?" Holmes asked.

The duke exclaimed, "Absolutely not!"

Holmes persisted. "Did you encourage him in your recent letter to leave the school?"

"No, sir!" exclaimed the duke.

"Did you send that letter yourself?" Holmes demanded.

Mr. Wilder broke in. "That is my job. I made sure it was sent."

And with that, the duke abruptly asked us to leave. "I'm very busy, gentlemen. But do keep me posted on your findings."

Huxtable had invited us to stay in some rooms at the school. So we went back there.

Later, Holmes left for several hours. He returned with a map of the area. He had also interviewed the neighborhood people.

Holmes and I studied the map closely.

We decided that the boy had to have traveled north. All things considered, it was the only option. Huxtable later confirmed our suspicions—

"We've found Arthur's hat!" he cried, entering our quarters. "A farmer found it up north. On the moors."

◼ Hot on the Trail

The next morning, we began our search of the moors. Soon, Holmes came upon some bicycle tracks.

"Hurrah!" I cried. "We have it!"

But Holmes shook his head. "These tracks are from a Dunlop tire," he explained. "With a patch on it. Heidegger's bike had Palmer tires. They leave different tracks."

"The boy's then?" I asked.

"Possibly. But we have no proof that he left on a bike," Holmes said.

We continued our search. Then Holmes let out a cry of delight. He'd found tracks made from Palmer tires!

So we followed the tracks. In a moment, the gleam of metal caught my eye. We dragged a bent-up bicycle from some thick bushes. It had Palmer tires. And the frame was splattered with blood.

We dug deeper into the bushes. There we found a body. The man wore shoes but no socks. And a nightshirt under his coat. Poor

Heidegger was dead! Apparently from a violent blow to the head.

"What shall we do, Watson?" explained Holmes. "We've lost so much time in tracking the boy. I feel that we should push on. But we must report Heidegger's death to the police."

"Wait!" I cried. "There is a fellow cutting moss up ahead. Perhaps he can go to the police."

We got the man's attention. He agreed to help.

Holmes sent him off to the police. And he gave him a note for Huxtable. Then we picked up the track of the other bike. It led us to an inn.

Mr. Reuben Hayes ran the inn. He greeted us roughly as we entered.

"No rooms tonight!" he barked.

"We were hoping just to rest for a bit," Holmes lied. "We're on our way to Holdernesse Hall. We have news about the duke's son."

This visibly startled Hayes. "Have you found him?" he asked.

"No," replied Holmes. "But there is news of him in Liverpool. They expect to find him soon."

Hayes smiled and appeared to relax. "May I offer you fellas some horses?" he said. "For the rest of your trip, I mean?"

"How kind," said Holmes. "But could you bring round a bicycle instead?"

"There's no bicycle here," Hayes declared. He disappeared, saying he'd fetch the horses soon. But we heard him go upstairs.

"Let's slip out while he's upstairs. Perhaps we can find something," whispered Holmes.

We crept out to the stable. There were two horses. And a stable boy. The lad didn't notice us. So he continued his work.

Suddenly, we heard Hayes' voice behind us. "You slippery spies!" he cried. "What are you doing?"

"Now, now, Mr. Hayes," said Holmes. "We're just having a look around. We thank you for your offer. But we're going to continue our journey on foot."

Hayes watched until we had left his property. We knew that Hayes was guilty of something. So we hid among the trees until all was clear. And we went back.

Just then, we saw a cyclist heading toward the inn. From the direction of Holdernesse Hall.

"Get down, Watson!" cried Holmes.

The man flew past us on the road. He did not see us.

"The duke's secretary!" I exclaimed.

We scrambled from rock to rock. Until we could see the front door of the inn. Wilder's bicycle was leaning against it.

The lights went out at the inn. Then we heard noises from the stable. And a carriage took off in the darkness.

"What do you make of that, Watson?" Holmes whispered.

"It looks like someone is fleeing," I said.

"Well, it certainly was not Mr. James Wilder," said Holmes. "For there he is at the door."

A second dark figure appeared by Wilder's side. Five minutes later, a lamp was lit in a first-floor window.

Together we stole down to the door of the inn. The bicycle still leaned against the wall. Holmes struck a match and held it to the back wheel. He chuckled at the sight of the patched Dunlop tire. Above us was the lighted window.

"I must have a peep," said Holmes.

Instantly, his feet were on my shoulders. He got down just as quickly.

"Come, my friend," said Holmes. "It's a long walk to the school. The sooner we get started the better."

■ Guilty as Charged

The next morning, Holmes and I visited the duke.

"Well, Mr. Holmes?" said the duke.

"Dr. Huxtable tells us that a reward has been offered in this case. Is this true?" Holmes asked.

"Yes," confirmed the duke. "Five thousand pounds to anyone who can tell me where my son is. And one thousand to the man who can identify the person who held him."

"Good," said Holmes. "Then I would ask you to write me a check for 6,000 pounds."

"Is this a joke?" asked the duke.

"Not at all," assured Holmes. "I know where your son is. And I know who is holding him."

"Where is he?" the duke gasped.

"He is at the Hayes Inn," revealed Holmes. "About two miles from your gate."

The duke fell back in his chair. "And whom do you accuse?" he asked.

Sherlock Holmes stepped swiftly forward. He touched the duke upon the shoulder. And he declared, "I accuse you."

The duke sprang to his feet. Then he sank back down. And he cradled his face in his hands. At last, he spoke—

"How much do you know?" he asked.

"I saw you last night," Holmes said. "Through the window. And I saw your son and James Wilder."

"Have you told anyone else?" the duke asked.

"I have spoken to no one," Holmes said.

The duke reached for a pen with trembling fingers. He filled out a check. "What if I gave you *12,000* pounds?"

Holmes smiled and shook his head. "I fear, sir, that matters cannot be arranged so easily. There is Heidegger's death to consider."

"But James never intended for that to happen!" cried the duke. "He had nothing to do with that. Hayes did it. You must save James! He is my son!"

"Mr. Wilder is your son?" I gasped.

To the duke, Holmes said, "I already notified the police about Hayes last night. They caught him this morning in Chesterfield. But now you must shed more light on your relationship with Mr. Wilder."

The duke took a deep breath. Then he told his story.

"You see, I was married before," the duke explained. "When I was very young. To a sweet, beautiful girl. We had a son—James. But my family was against the marriage.

"They forced my wife to move far away. Then they drew up papers that said the marriage never existed. And that James was not a true heir to the family's fortune. I was heartbroken.

"After his mother died, James found me," the duke continued. "I hired him as my private secretary. But in the eyes of the law, he has no rights in the family. He hates me for that. He hates young Arthur even more.

"My wife, the current Duchess of Holdernesse, knows all this. I knew that James was full of hatred for us all. And I became afraid for my wife's safety. And Arthur's.

"So I sent my wife to the south of France. And I told people that we were not getting along. Then I put Arthur in the Priory School.

"I did send Arthur a letter. But James destroyed it and sent a different note. It told Arthur to leave the school in the middle of the night. To meet James in the nearby woods. The note said that James would take Arthur to his mother."

The duke took a deep breath and continued. "Arthur trusted James. So he did as he was told.

"James bicycled over and spoke to Arthur. He told him to wait for Hayes, who would take him by horseback to his mother's side.

"Meanwhile, Heidegger had been unable to sleep that night. He was staring out his window. And he saw Arthur walking into the woods. By the time Heidegger was able to take off on his bike, Hayes had picked up Arthur. And when Heidegger caught up with them, Hayes struck him with a stick.

"Hayes then took Arthur to his inn. When James heard about Heidegger, he came to me and confessed. He wanted nothing to do with murder. He begged for my forgiveness. And my help.

"He explained that he had kidnapped Arthur. And that he'd planned to leak this scandal to the papers. Unless I found a way to will my entire estate to him. He knew I would never turn him in to the police. How could I? But he hadn't counted on Heidegger's murder.

"I agreed to provide Hayes with a carriage to escape in. That, in exchange for my dear Arthur."

Holmes broke in. "You have covered up a crime. And you have helped a murderer escape. True?"

The duke hung his head as an answer.

"This is a most serious matter, sir," scolded Holmes. "Not to mention that you now know where Arthur is. And you haven't brought him home! All to help your older son? Cad that he is? This is most unpleasant."

"I know, Holmes," said the duke softly. "I have done poorly by both my sons."

Holmes went on. "I will help you. If you ring for a servant. And you must let me give such orders as I like."

Without a word, the duke rang the bell. A servant entered.

"You will be glad to hear this," said Holmes. "Young Arthur has been found. The duke wishes you to bring him home. He is at the Hayes Inn."

Holmes turned back to the duke.

"Now I am not in an official position," he offered. "But as long as the ends of justice are served, I will not repeat all that I know."

The duke was relieved.

"The gallows await Hayes," continued Holmes. "The police will think that he kidnapped the boy for ransom. I have no doubt that you can convince Hayes to stay silent. The police are unlikely, then, to put the other pieces together."

"Quite right," I agreed. "The trail is too cold now."

"Furthermore!" exclaimed Holmes, slapping the table. "You should have nothing more to do with James. And you should bring the duchess back home at once."

"Agreed!" vowed the duke.

"Now, Watson," said Holmes. "Let us take our leave."

"Yes, let's," I agreed.

"There's just one more thing," said Holmes. He pointed to a watercolor behind the desk. And he addressed the duke. "Tell me, sir, where did you find that marvelous painting?"

The duke, a bit flustered, answered, "Why, in Paris."

"It's lovely," said Holmes. "It is the second most interesting object I have seen in the North."

"And the first?" inquired the duke.

Holmes scooped the check for 12,000 pounds from the desktop. He folded it up.

"I am a poor man," said he. Then he patted the check affectionately. And he thrust it into the safety of his inner pocket.

THE THREE STUDENTS

The Play

Cast of Characters

Narrator
Soames
Watson
Holmes
Bannister
Gilchrist
McLaren

Setting: The College of St. Luke's in 1895

Act One

Narrator: Sherlock Holmes and Dr. Watson each had research to do. So they decided to spend some time at The College of St. Luke's.

One evening, Professor Soames visited them in their guest quarters. He was an old friend of both. And he was in desperate need of their help.

Soames: I do hope you can spare me a few hours of your time. Something terrible has happened. And I don't know what to do.

Watson: Whatever is the matter, Soames?

Holmes: Pray tell!

Soames: As you know, I teach Greek. I am giving an important test tomorrow. It's a competition. The student with the highest score will win an award.

I went out this afternoon. And I left the test on my desk. I was gone for an hour. When I returned, a key was in my door. I had my own with me. So I realized that my butler must have left his in the door by mistake.

I rang for him. And he apologized. He had entered my room to see if I wanted tea. When he found me absent, he carelessly left the key behind.

Holmes: I'm afraid I don't see the problem, dear fellow.

Soames: Of course. I shall get to the point. The two of us looked about my room. I looked at my desk. And my blood ran cold. Someone had looked through my papers! The test was on three pages. I had left them together. Now one of them was on the floor. One was on a table near the window. And the third was still on the desk.

Holmes: Fascinating!

Watson: Very. Please go on.

Soames: I must conclude that one of the students has tried to cheat.

Holmes: What about your butler—Bannister, isn't it? Did he touch the papers?

Soames: He swears he did not. And I believe him. Bannister has been with me for ten years. He is an honest man with a noble character.

Besides, Bannister was very upset. He nearly fainted. He sat down to rest while I examined the room.

Watson: What did you find?

Soames: Several things. On the table were shreds from a sharpened pencil. A broken tip of lead was there too. The rascal must have copied the test in a hurry.

Holmes: Excellent! Fortune has been your friend.

Soames: Also, the top of my desk is covered with red leather. There is a new three-inch cut in it. And I found a tiny ball of black clay. I am convinced that these marks were left by the intruder. There was no other evidence. Can you help me?

Holmes: Gladly. Tell me—did anyone visit you after the test was prepared?

Soames: Yes. Ras did. He's a student from India. He came in to ask me a question.

Watson: Were the papers on your table?

Soames: Yes. But they were rolled up. He could not have known what they were.

Holmes: Did anyone know that the test would be in your room?

Soames: No one.

Holmes: Where is Bannister now?

Soames: I left him in the chair. I was in such a hurry to find you. All I had time to do was lock up the papers.

Holmes: Let us investigate!

Act Two

Narrator: Professor Soames led the others to his quarters. His room was on the ground floor. Above him were three students—one on each floor. It was already dusk when the group reached the building.

Holmes studied the professor's window. Then he stood on tiptoe. With his neck craned, he looked into the room.

Soames: He must have entered through the door. No man could fit through this window.

Holmes: Right you are.

Narrator: Soames ushered Holmes and Watson inside. Holmes examined the carpet.

Holmes: You say you left Bannister in a chair. Which one?

Soames: By the window.

Holmes: I see. Near this little table. Clearly, the intruder took the pages, one by one, from the desk. Then he carried them to this table.

Watson: Whatever for?

Holmes: Because from there he could see out. If Soames came across the yard, he could escape.

Soames: But I entered by the side door.

Holmes: Ah, so you surprised him. He panicked. He threw down the paper he was copying. Then he hid himself.

Narrator: Holmes studied the pencil shavings.

Holmes: Take note of this, Watson. His pencil was large. It had a soft lead. The outer color was dark blue. The brand name was printed in silver lettering. The intruder also had a large, blunt knife with him. That's how he sharpened the pencil.

Narrator: Soames and Watson exchanged looks. They were amazed at Holmes' cleverness.

Holmes: Now for the central table . . . and this black clay . . . and the tear in the leather. May I glance around your bedroom?

Soames: Of course.

Narrator: Soames showed Holmes the way.

Holmes: What's this? Aha! Another piece of clay. The intruder must have hidden in here.

Soames: Good gracious! The intruder was here when I was? Even while I spoke to Bannister?

Holmes: So it seems. Now—you said that there are three students who live in this building. So they all regularly pass your door. Are they all taking your test?

Soames: Yes.

Holmes: Tell me about them.

Soames: Gilchrist is one. He's a fine scholar. He should do well on the test. He's an athlete too. He won medals for the hurdles and the long jump.

Holmes: So he's a tall fellow?

Soames: Yes—quite. Then there's Ras. He lives on the second floor. Greek is his weak subject. But he works hard.

The top floor belongs to McLaren. He is brilliant. But quite lazy. He hasn't studied a bit all term.

Watson: Do you suspect him?

Soames: He seems the most likely.

Holmes: Of course. Bring in Bannister, please.

Narrator: Soames rang the bell. Bannister rushed in. He looked nervous and upset.

Bannister: How may I help you, sirs?

Soames: Holmes would like to ask you a few questions.

Bannister: Very well. I feel just terrible about leaving the key in the door.

Soames: Naturally, old boy. Nobody blames you.

Holmes: When did you enter the room?

Bannister: Half-past four. The professor was not home. So I left at once.

Holmes: You were upset when you found out what had happened. Correct?

Bannister: Yes, sir. I nearly fainted. Such a terrible thing.

Holmes: Why did you sit in the chair near

the corner? Weren't these other chairs closer to you?

Bannister: I don't know, sir. It didn't matter to me where I sat.

Narrator: Holmes studied Bannister's face closely. Bannister shifted on his feet. Droplets of sweat appeared on his brow.

Soames: I really don't think Bannister knows anything, Holmes.

Holmes: We shall move on, then, Soames. May I meet the students?

Soames: Easily.

Narrator: Soames led the way to Gilchrist's door.

Holmes: No names, please!

Soames: Naturally. We show people round the campus all the time. He'll think this is a tour.

Narrator: Soames knocked. Gilchrist invited them in.

Holmes: A pleasure to meet you. Goodness, you are very tall!

Gilchrist: Yes, sir. I'm six-foot-five.

Narrator: Holmes looked about the room. He admired a piece of art. And he insisted upon sketching it in his notebook. He asked to borrow a pencil. Gilchrist gave him one. Then Holmes broke the lead. He borrowed a knife to sharpen it.

Holmes repeated these actions in Ras' room.

Then Soames led them to McLaren's room. He knocked on the door.

McLaren: Go away! And don't come back! I'm trying to study!

Soames: How rude. Of course, he doesn't know who knocked.

Narrator: Holmes' next question seemed odd to the others.

Holmes: Can you tell me his exact height?

Soames: Really, Holmes, I don't understand your logic. But I would say he is taller than Ras. And not so tall as Gilchrist. Perhaps five-foot-ten.

Holmes: And I am exactly six feet tall. That is very important. And now, I shall say good night.

Soames: But you cannot leave now! The test is tomorrow. I cannot give the test if someone has the answers. The situation must be faced.

Holmes: You must trust me. I will take the clay and the pencil cuttings with me. I'll know more in the morning. Meanwhile, stick to your plans.

Soames: Very good.

Narrator: Holmes and Watson walked across the campus.

Watson: Any ideas, my friend?

Holmes: That Bannister fellow puzzles me. He seems a perfectly honest man. But something doesn't fit. Ah—here's a supply shop. Let's pop in.

Narrator: Holmes and Watson stopped at four supply shops that evening. They could not find a pencil to match the shavings. But Holmes was not discouraged.

Holmes: I have one more idea, Watson. I'll look into that first thing tomorrow.

Act Three

Narrator: Holmes and Watson set off at eight the next morning.

Watson: You seem in good spirits. Have you have formed a conclusion?

Holmes: Yes, my dear Watson. I have solved the mystery!

Narrator: Holmes showed Watson three little clay balls.

Watson: What's this? Yesterday, there were only two.

Holmes: I visited the athletic fields at dawn. This clay is found in the jumping pit. The athletes wear spiked shoes. And balls of clay often stick to the spikes.

Watson: Gilchrist!

Holmes: Indeed. We shall inform Soames at once.

Narrator: Soames met his friends at the door. He all but pounced on them!

Soames: What have you found? Shall I give the test?

Holmes: By all means. But Gilchrist is out of the running. Ring the bell for Bannister. And all will become clear.

Narrator: Bannister entered. He looked sick at heart. He could not speak.

Holmes then shared his conclusions with the group.

Holmes: I know all about it, Bannister. You sat in the corner chair to conceal something. Then Mr. Soames left the room. And you released the intruder. He'd been hiding in that bedroom.

Narrator: Bannister turned ghostly white.

Holmes: Please remain in the room. Stand over there. That's right, near the bedroom door.

Soames, please fetch Gilchrist.

Narrator: An instant later, Soames returned. Gilchrist's troubled blue eyes rested upon Bannister.

Gilchrist: How could you?

Bannister: I never said a word! I swear!

Holmes: Ah, but now you have both given yourselves away.

Gilchrist, you have only one hope. And that is to confess to your deeds at once.

Narrator: Gilchrist began to sob. He was clearly ashamed.

Holmes: Come, come—it is human to err. At least no one can accuse you of being a hard criminal. Collect yourself. And I will confess for you.

Soames: Do tell me what happened!

Holmes: When I approached your room, Soames, I studied the window. Only a very tall man would be able to see your desk from the outside. He would have to be taller than I.

Gilchrist had been practicing the jump yesterday afternoon. He returned carrying his jumping shoes. They have several sharp spikes.

As he passed your window, he saw the papers on your table. And he guessed they were for the test. Then he saw the key in your door. He could not resist! So he entered the room and looked at the test.

Gilchrist—what did you put on that chair near the window?

Gilchrist: Gloves.

Holmes: Of course! He put his gloves on the chair. And he started to copy the test. But he was surprised by your return, Soames. He forgot his gloves. But he grabbed his shoes and darted into the bedroom. The scratch on that table is from the shoes. And the clay fell off the spikes—one ball near the desk. And one ball in the bedroom.

Have I told the truth, Mr. Gilchrist?

Gilchrist: Yes, sir.

Soames: Good heavens, Gilchrist! Have you nothing to add?

Gilchrist: Yes, sir. I am dreadfully sorry, sir. But I had decided not to take the test. I could not go through with it. I have been offered a job in South Africa. With the Rhodesian police. And I am going to take it. It is Bannister who set me on the right path.

Holmes: Come now, Bannister. Clearly, you sat on the gloves. And you protected young Gilchrist. Please clear up the last point in this mystery. What were your reasons?

Bannister: I used to be the butler to Gilchrist's father. He was a great man.

After he died, I found work at the college. I watched over young Gilchrist for the sake of the old days.

Yesterday, we realized that the test had been tampered with. I saw the tan gloves in that chair. I recognized them. And I guessed what had happened.

I flung myself into that chair. Nothing would budge me. Not until Mr. Soames left the room.

Then out came Gilchrist. And he confessed it all to me.

Narrator: Bannister paused. He looked Soames, then Holmes, then Watson in the face.

Bannister: Wasn't it natural, sirs, for me to save him? I took care of him when he was a baby! I felt it my duty to try to guide him. To prevent him from cheating on that test. Can you blame me?

Holmes: No, indeed!

Well, Soames, I think we have cleared up your little problem. Our breakfast awaits us. Come, Watson!

And you, Gilchrist! I trust that a bright future awaits you in Rhodesia. You have already fallen low. Let us see, in the future, how high you can rise!

DATE DUE

MAR 27 2001			
NOV 2 7 2002			
930			

SC
Owe

Owens, L   L.

Tales of Sherlock
Holmes